For Darcy and
the Kent Street playground
A. S.

For the sandpit kids at
Hawthorn Kinder
B. G.

Text copyright © 2018 by Ann Stott
Illustrations copyright © 2018 by Blackbird Pty. Ltd.

First edition 2018

Library of Congress Catalog Card Number pending
ISBN 978-0-7636-8173-9

18 19 20 21 22 23 LEO 10 9 8 7 6 5 4 3 2 1

Printed in Heshan, Guangdong, China

This book was typeset in Journal.
The illustrations were done in watercolor.

Candlewick Press
99 Dover Street
Somerville, Massachusetts 02144

visit us at www.candlewick.com

Want to
Play Trucks?

Ann Stott
illustrated by Bob Graham

CANDLEWICK PRESS

Jack and Alex meet almost every morning
in the sandbox at Atwood playground.

Jack likes trucks.

Alex likes dolls.

Jack likes big trucks that can wreck things.

Alex likes dolls with pink, sparkly dresses.

"Want to play trucks?" asks Jack.

"Let's play dolls . . .

that drive trucks," says Alex.

So Jack and Alex play dolls that drive trucks.

"I like trucks that have loud sirens," says Jack.

"I like dolls that dance and wear tutus," says Alex.

"I like trucks that have cranes that can reach way up high to the very top of a burning building," says Jack.

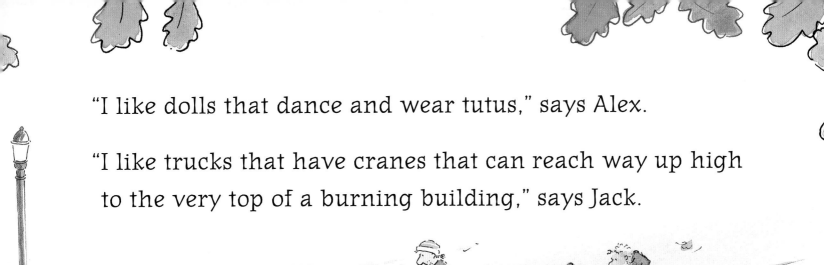

"I like dolls that can do dips and twirls," sings Alex.
"My doll can spin way up high in the clouds."

"You can't wear a tutu and drive a crane," says Jack.

"Yes, you can," says Alex.

"No, you can't!" demands Jack.

"YES," says Alex.

"NO!" shouts Jack.

"YES, YOU CAN!" shouts Alex.

"No, you can't," says Jack. "It wouldn't fit in the driver's seat."

"Oh," says Alex. "Then overalls.
Purple overalls."

"VAROOM!
VAROOM!"

"I like trucks that carry lots of stuff," says Jack.

Ding Ding Ding Ding

"I like dolls that drive ice-cream trucks!" says Alex.

"Do you like ice cream?" asks Alex.

"I like ice cream!" shouts Jack.

"WE LIKE

ICE CREAM!"